# There's a Giraffe in My Soup

by Ross Burach

**HARPER**

*An Imprint of HarperCollinsPublishers*

Library of Congress Control Number: 2015932003
ISBN 978-0-06-236014-4

The artist used pencil and acrylic paints colored digitally to create the illustrations for this book.
Typography by Dana Fritts
17 18 19   SCP   10 9 8 7 6 5 4 3

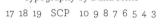

First Edition

*For Polly and Mom*

Excuse me, waiter?

There's a **giraffe** in my soup!

*This is a fine restaurant, sir.*
*That simply cannot be.*

# Look at that!

There **is** a giraffe in your soup!

*A new bowl of soup for you, right away!*

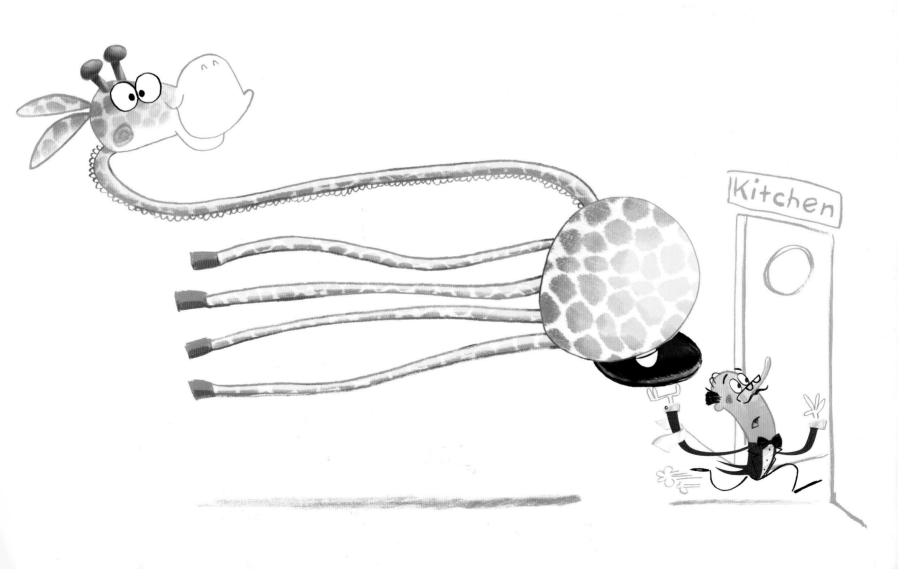

Here you are, sir. A fresh bowl of soup.
Minus the giraffe, of course. Bon appétit.

# Hello, little frog.

How did you get in my soup?

A new **Chomp!** *bowl of soup for you* **Chomp!** *right away!*

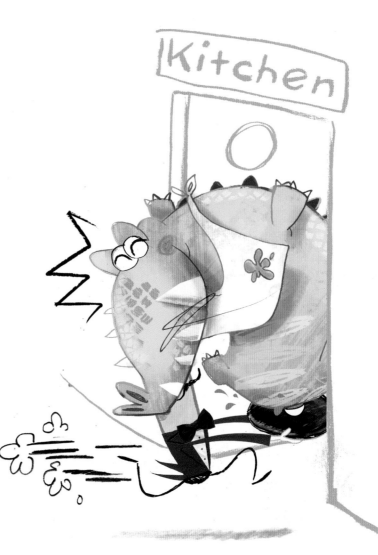

Here you are, sir. A new bowl of soup.
Alligator-free. Enjoy.

Waiter! Waiter! **Save her! Save her!** Please hurry!

There's an **elephant** in my soup,

and I don't think she can swim!

Waiter! Waiter!
Hurry back!

**Yak!
Yak!
Yak!**

*Yuck?
Yuck?
Yuck?*

Oh.
**YAK.**
Yuck.

Walrus!

Ostrich!

Shh . . . koala.

Snake!

Burp

Whale!

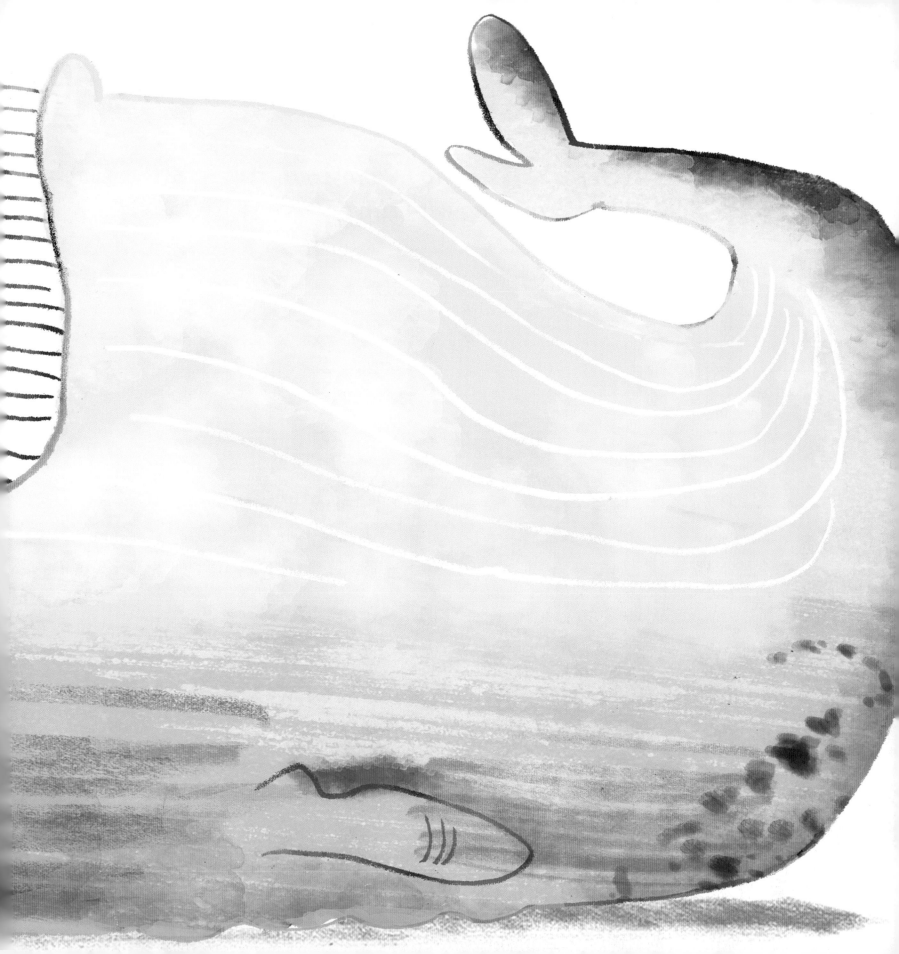

Here, *huff* at last. Your soup, *huff* roaring with flavor.

*Lying? Lying? Lying?*
*Enough of your complaints!*
*Sure, I made a minor gaffe*
*with the giraffe.*

**Maybe** *I overlooked a whale.*

*But when it comes to taste,*
*I am a professional. Do not*
*dare accuse me of ...*

*I am terribly sorry, sir. It seems there's been a slight mix-up. The zoo was sent our food, and we were sent their animals.*

Let's skip the soup.
Maybe dessert?

*Dessert is our treat!*

One mousse . . . with a cherry on top!

hop
hop

Never mind! I'm eating
somewhere else!

Wait for me!

Table for one?